I COME IN PEACE

Adapted from the film by Jan Carr

DISNEP PRESS

New York

CONTENTS

FROM

Disney's

TOY STORY

★ I COME IN PEACE ★

1. ✴ THE ENEMY PLANET

It's not easy being a space ranger. A space ranger has to travel to new planets. If his ship is damaged on the trip, he'll have trouble returning home. He might even find himself on an enemy planet, where the people try to hurt him.

This is exactly what happened to me. Or so I thought. Later I'd learn the truth. Woody and I would piece together the whole, long story. But that would be much later, after he and I finally got a chance to sit down and talk together as friends.

Our story starts on Andy's birthday. Andy is a boy, and he was turning six. He lives in a house with his mom, his little sister, Molly, and lots and lots of toys. When I arrived, Andy brought me to his room and placed me on his bed. The creatures in his room were staring at me. One was a cowboy. Another was a potato. There was a dinosaur, a piggy bank, and a dog made of a stretchy, metal coil. That one was called Slinky. None of them looked very friendly.

"Greetings!" I said. "I am Buzz Lightyear. I come in peace."

The cowboy looked me up and down. His name was Woody, and he was Andy's favorite toy.

"We are all impressed with Andy's new *toy*," he said. Was he talking about me? He certainly didn't sound impressed.

"I'm not a toy," I told him. "I'm a space ranger. I protect the galaxy from the evil emperor, Zurg. He is our sworn enemy."

Woody laughed.

I pressed a button on my chest. Out popped my space wings.

"Those wings are plastic," sneered Woody. "You can't fly."

"Can," I told him.

"Can't," he insisted.

"I could fly around this room with my eyes closed," I said.

"Prove it," he shot back.

I stepped to the edge of the bed and leaped off. "To infinity and beyond!" I cried.

Whee! I bounced onto a ball, and I bounced back up, landing in a car. The car sped down a track and shot me into the air. I *was* flying! I caught hold of a mobile and swung neatly back over the bed, landing directly in front of Woody.

"Can!" I said triumphantly.

"That wasn't flying," he snapped. "That was falling with style."

The cowboy was just jealous; that much was clear. But I had no time for such worries. I was a space ranger. I had to fix my ship. The other toys gathered around to help me, but Woody stuck his face right up in mine, threatening me.

"Listen, Lightsnack," he said. "You stay away from Andy. He's mine, and no one is taking him away from me."

"Would you like to lodge a complaint with the star command?" I asked.

Woody's face flushed with anger. He lunged at me and tore open my helmet. Air rushed into my nostrils. I choked, trying to catch my breath.

"How dare you!" I cried. "I am on an uncharted planet! What if the air had been toxic?"

Woody stared at me. "You actually think you're the *real* Buzz Lightyear?" he asked. "You're a toy!" He spelled it out for me: "T-O-Y!"

Suddenly, outside, a dog barked. The toys raced to the window to look out. A boy was in the yard next door. He was strapping one of his army men to a firecracker. This looked like trouble.

"That's Sid," said Woody.

"He tortures toys," explained Rex, the dinosaur. "Just for fun."

"We've got to do something!" I cried.

Bang! The sound of an explosion rattled the window and shook the room. Sid had

blown up the army man!

Andy's toys backed away from the window.

"Andy and his family are moving soon," said Bo Peep. "We'll go with them and get away from Sid. The sooner we leave, the better."

The next day, Andy began packing for the move. As he sorted through his toys, his mother peeked into the room.

"You can finish when we get back from Pizza Planet," she told Andy.

"Pizza Planet!" cried Andy. "Cool! Can I bring some toys?"

"You can bring *one* toy," his mother decided. "Go wash your hands first."

Andy raced out of the room. Woody glared at me.

"Hey, Buzz," he called. "There's trouble outside! A helpless toy! It's trapped behind the dresser!"

A helpless toy! There was no time to lose! I ran to help.

"I don't see anything," I said.

But when I turned to Woody, I did see trouble. A car was heading toward me. Woody held the remote control. He was aiming the car directly at me! I dove out of the way, but a lamp swung toward me, knocking me out the window.

The toys stared out the window, trying to find me.

"Woody *pushed* him!" cried Mr. Potato Head.

I was stranded on a strange planet, stuck in a thick hedge of prickly bushes.

As I said, it isn't easy being a space ranger. I'd landed in enemy territory. And I had no idea how I was going to get back to my ship, or how I was going to get home.

2. ✷ SID'S HOUSE

Soon Andy came out of the house. He had Woody in his hand. "I couldn't find Buzz," I heard him say to his mother. He and his family piled into their van.

When the van pulled past the bushes, I grabbed the fender and jumped aboard. I held on tight as the van moved out into traffic. Andy's mom drove into what looked like a fuel depot. When she and Andy stepped out of their van, I jumped inside.

 Woody was surprised to see me.

"Buzz!" he cried. "You're alive! This is great! You can tell all the toys that the fall was an accident. Right?"

Accident? Hardly! I lunged at Woody. We fell off the seat and bounced out of the door. Woody pounded my chest. I set his head spinning. As Woody and I were rolling around on the ground fighting, Andy and his mom got back into the van. Andy shut the door. His mom started the engine. Woody and I sat up and stared as the van pulled out of the fuel depot without us. Once again, I was stranded. And this time, I had *no* idea where I was.

I flipped open my wrist communicator.

"Buzz Lightyear, mission log," I said. I looked around. "I seem to be at a refueling station of some sort."

"Shut up, you idiot!" cried Woody. "This is all your fault!"

"My fault?" I shouted back. "Because of you, the security of the entire universe is in danger! You have delayed my rendezvous with the star command!"

"Star command?" Woody laughed at me. "What are you talking about? You're a *toy!* An action figure! A child's plaything!"

A space ranger has no time to listen to such nonsense. I stalked off. I had to search for some sort of craft to get me home.

"Buzz!" Woody called me back. "I found a spaceship!"

I turned around. Woody was standing next to a vehicle with four wheels. It had what looked like a rocket ship on top and it seemed to be in the process of refueling.

 "This spaceship will take us to Pizza Planet," Woody told me. "Then you can

find another ship to
take you home."

"Okay," I agreed.
"Let's climb aboard,"
and I strapped myself
in. Woody sat in the

back of the vehicle but he got knocked
around because he didn't strap himself in.

But, as Woody had promised, the space-
craft drove us to a place called Pizza Planet.

"My stars!"
I exclaimed.
All around,
bells were
chiming and
lights were

blinking on and off. Pizza Planet must be
some sort of mission control! Woody walked

15

off to look for Andy, but I had to find a space-ship. I spied one across the room and climbed aboard. The ship was packed with aliens.

"I need to take over your ship," I told them. "Who's in charge here?"

The aliens pointed to a claw that swung above us, which was attached to a crane.

Woody had followed me. "Buzz, what are you *doing?*" he cried. He looked up at the claw.

"The claw is our master," the aliens told us.

"Oh brother," Woody muttered.

Someone walked up to the ship. It was Sid. Andy's neighbor! He fished some quarters out of his pocket, dropped them in a slot, and pulled a lever. The claw swung toward us.

"Get down!" Woody shouted. He dove into the pile of aliens, but the claw was already swinging down. It grabbed me by my helmet. Woody clutched my feet, trying to hold me back, but the claw lifted both of us high out of the pile.

"Gotcha!" cried Sid. "Cool." He grinned when he saw me. "A Buzz Lightyear!"

He stuck us in his backpack and took us home.

It is hard to describe Sid's house. It was more like a nightmare than a home. As we came through the door, Sid grabbed a doll away from his sister, Hannah.

"This doll is sick!" he told her. "I have to perform an operation!"

"No!" Hannah shrieked. "Don't touch her!"

But Sid had already run upstairs. He tossed his backpack on his bed. Woody and I peered out.

As we watched, Sid ripped the head off the doll. He stuck a dinosaur head in its place.

"There," he said to Hannah. "She's all better now."

"Mom!" screeched Hannah. She tore down the stairs. Sid ran after her. Woody and I leaped out of the backpack.

"We're going to die!" cried Woody. He ran for the door to try to escape. It was locked!

Something rustled in the shadows. We could see an eye peering out from under the bed. It looked like it belonged to a baby doll.

"Hey there," Woody called to the doll. "Do you know a way out of here?"

The creature crawled out from under the bed. It wasn't a doll at all! The doll's head was

stuck on a spider-like body! Its legs were long, sharp, and metal.

All around, other creatures crawled out from the shadows. All of them were mutants, with body parts that Sid had mixed up. There was a fishing reel with doll's legs, a skateboard with a head, and a car with arms. The creatures picked up Hannah's doll and

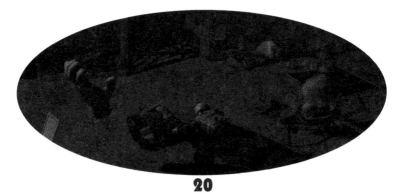

dragged it under the bed. They grabbed the dinosaur body and carried it off into the shadows.

Woody and I looked on in horror. What were they going to do? Were they going to eat the toys?

"They're cannibals!" I cried.

Woody and I bolted across the room and jumped into the backpack. We zipped it tightly over our heads.

"Mayday!" I cried. I jiggled the communicator on my wrist. "Come in, star command! Send reinforcements! Do you hear me?"

I checked my laser. It blinked and blipped. I knew I'd better check *all* my weapons. If the star command didn't show up, Woody and I would have to fight off these creatures by ourselves!

3. ✵ AM I JUST A TOY?

Sid was not gone for long. He was back soon enough, looking for trouble. He picked up Woody, threw him against the wall, and pretended to question him.

Then Sid opened his window shade and bright sunlight shone into his room. I was horrified when I saw him pick up a magnifying glass and focus it on Woody. A bright white-hot dot formed on Woody's forehead and it began to burn. Luckily, Sid's mother called him.

As soon as he left the room, we ran for the door. We might have made it, but the mutant toys jumped in our path, blocking our way. I fired my laser at them. Nothing happened.

"The laser should work!" I cried. "I recharged it before I left!"

"You idiot!" shouted Woody. "You're a *toy!*"

Woody grabbed me from behind and

pressed a button on my back. My arm flew out in a karate chop.

"Get back!" Woody cried to the mutant toys. "Get back!"

We fought our way to the door, then ran down the hall. Sid's dog, Scud, was lying on the landing of the stairway, snoring. I ran past him and Woody followed, but Woody's pull string caught on the railing. As he crept forward, the string snapped back.

"Yeee-haw!" Oh no! Woody's voice box! It woke up the dog! Scud's eyes shot open. He growled.

"Giddyap, pardner!" Woody's voice box sounded again. "We've got to get this wagon train moving!"

Scud bounded up the stairs and chased after us. I ran through a door. Woody hid in a closet, slamming the door behind him. Scud barked and scratched at the door.

Suddenly, I heard a voice. "Calling Buzz Lightyear!" it said. "This is the star command!"

The star command! I stepped toward the voice. It was coming from a box with moving

pictures. I'd find out later that the box was called a television set.

"Buzz Lightyear," it said. "Do you read me?"

"Yes!" I was about to shout, but someone answered for me. It was someone else on the screen of the television set. A boy was playing with a toy, and the toy looked like *me*.

"Yes, kids," continued the announcer. "The world's greatest superhero is now the world's greatest toy."

Toy?

"He has karate-chop action, a laser light, a voice simulator . . . and he even has space wings!"

Laser light? Karate chop? Space wings? Those were all the things *I* had. Could it be? Was Woody right? Maybe I wasn't a space ranger after all. Maybe I *was* just a toy. A silly, useless toy.

I knew one way to find out. I climbed up the railing of the stairs. If I *was* a space ranger, I'd be able to fly. I leaped off the railing.

"To infinity and beyond!" I cried.

But I didn't fly. I crashed to the floor below. I looked around, stunned. My arm had fallen off! As I lay there, helpless, Sid's little sister walked by. She picked me up and took me to her room. There, she set me in a chair

with her dolls. They were having a tea party.

So it had come to this. I was only a toy—
a toy at a tea party.

"Buzz!" called Woody. "Are you okay?"

I didn't answer. What was the use? One
minute I'm defending the galaxy and suddenly I'm drinking tea with headless dolls.
Years of Academy training—wasted! Woody
grabbed me and shook me.

"Snap out of it, Buzz!" he said, "I think you've had enough tea." He had a plan. "This way!"

Woody had spied the window in Sid's room and Sid was nowhere in sight. The coast was clear! Woody ran to the window and pried it open. Across the yard was Andy's window. He could see Andy's toys! Woody waved to them.

"Hey!" he called. "Hey, guys!"

"Look!" they shouted back. "There's Woody! He's in Sid's bedroom! What are you doing there?" they asked.

Woody tossed them a string of Christmas lights.

"We're going to get out of here!" he called to me.

But Andy's toys were not ready to help.

Mr. Potato Head remembered that Woody had tried to run me over with the car. He grabbed the string of lights from Slinky.

"No!" Woody tried to explain. "Buzz is all right! Really! He's right here with me!"

Woody waved to me from the window. "Buzz," he urged, "give me a hand! Show the toys that you're not dead!"

I sat glumly on the floor. *If Woody wants a hand,* I thought, *I'll give him one.* I tossed him

my broken arm.

When the toys saw Woody with my arm, they screamed in shock. "Murderer!"

They dropped the lights and shut

the blinds, refusing to help. Once again, we were alone in Sid's bedroom, with no hope of help.

"Thanks a lot, Buzz," Woody snapped. "Why didn't you help me?"

Woody was so busy shouting at me, he didn't see the mutant toys. They were crawling out from the shadows, inching toward me. Before Woody could stop them, they fell on me. I thought that this would be the end of me. The mutant toys would drag me under the bed and eat me, just as they had eaten Hannah's doll. But the toys didn't drag me off, and they didn't eat me. Before Woody could fight them off, they stuck my arm back in its socket. They fixed me! With them were the dinosaur and Hannah's doll. The mutants had fixed them, too! These toys were actually friendly! They weren't cannibals at all!

The sound of footsteps sent the toys scurrying under the bed. Someone was coming into the room. Oh no! It was Sid! In his arms he held a big package. Woody scrambled under a milk crate, but I stayed where I was, in the middle of the floor. I still didn't care what happened to me.

Sid tore open the package. Inside was a rocket.

"The Big One!" Sid cried. "It finally came!"

He spied me on the floor, snatched me up, and taped me to the rocket.

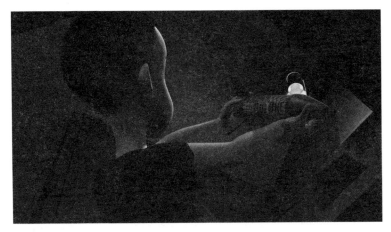

"To infinity and beyond!" he cried.

With that, he grabbed some matches and ran for the door.

So this was it. I would be blown to bits. I closed my eyes, waiting for the end.

But outside, the sky had darkened and thunder sounded.

"Oh no!" said Sid. He stopped and looked out the window. Rain was coming down in sheets.

"Well," Sid decided, "I'll do the launch

tomorrow when I wake up."

Sid slapped me down on the desk and climbed into bed. He set his alarm clock.

"Sweet dreams," he told me.

He clicked off the light. The room was pitched into darkness. I squirmed. The tape felt tight around my waist and the rocket was heavy. I couldn't escape! Tomorrow would be the end of me for sure.

4. ✶ THE GREAT ESCAPE

The next morning, as the sun rose, Woody called to me. He was trapped under the milk crate and needed my help to escape.

"I can't help you," I said sadly. "I can't help *anyone*. You were right all along. I'm not a space ranger. I'm only a toy. A stupid little toy."

"Hey. Whoa!" said Woody. "Wait a minute. Being a toy is a lot better than being a space ranger."

"Right," I laughed. Woody was trying to cheer me up, but I wasn't in the mood to be cheery.

"It *is*," Woody insisted. He nodded toward Andy's window. "Look. Over in that house is a kid who thinks that you're the greatest. And it's not because you're a space ranger. It's because you're a *toy!* You're *his* toy."

I didn't believe him. "Why would Andy want me?" I asked.

"Are you kidding?" Woody said. "You have wings! You light up! You can talk!"

The wings I had were *toy* wings. My lights were only *toy* lights.

"You're much better than I am," Woody went on. "I can't do any of the things you can. Now that Andy has you, he'll never want to play with me anymore."

Woody seemed sad, even sadder than I was. I didn't think Andy would want to play with me, but I was sure that he'd want Woody. Woody was his favorite toy. They'd played together for years.

I hopped to my feet and knocked over the crate.

"Come on, Sheriff!" I said. "There's a kid over there who needs us. Let's get you out."

Outside, a big truck pulled into Andy's driveway. It was a moving truck! That meant it was moving day!

"We've got to get out of here!" I cried to Woody. "Now!"

B-r-r-r-r-r-i-i-ing! Too late! Sid's alarm rang loudly. He woke with a start and jumped out of bed. Before we could hide, Sid grabbed me up and ran out of the room.

"Time for the Big One!" he cackled. He headed for the yard.

Woody tried to follow, but Scud was at the door. Woody slammed the door on the barking dog. How would he get out now?

The mutant toys moved out from under the bed. As Woody told me later, it was then that he got his idea. These toys could help him!

"We've got to save Buzz!" Woody urged. The toys huddled around Woody as he whispered his plan. They nodded and murmured.

"Let's do it!" they agreed.

Two of the toys dashed off. They squeezed through the heating duct and made their way through the walls. When they came to the porch outside, they rang the doorbell.

"I'll get it!" cried Hannah.

When Hannah opened the door, no one

was there. Scud ran between her legs, barking at the sound. Hannah shut the door, locking Scud outside.

With Scud gone, the coast was clear. Woody jumped on the skateboard with Roller

Bob, Babyface, and, the other mutant toys. They rolled through the kitchen and barreled out the small pet door that led outdoors. There, Woody spied me in the grass. I was stuck on a pole, the rocket still strapped to my back. Sid was getting ready to launch me.

But Woody had a plan. He lay down in the grass, where Sid could see him. Sid squinted. What was the cowboy doing outside? He picked Woody up and stuck a match in the cowboy's pocket.

"You and I will have a cookout later," he laughed, and he tossed Woody on the grill.

Then he struck another match and started the countdown. He was going to light the rocket!

"Ten! Nine! Eight! Seven! Six! Five! Four! Three! Two! One!"

Just as Sid was about to touch the match to the fuse, Woody spoke up. "Reach for the sky," he said.

Sid stopped cold. "Huh?" he asked.

"This town ain't big enough for the two of us," Woody said louder.

Sid walked to the grill. He picked up

Woody and turned him in his hands. The voice sounded as if it was coming from Woody's voice box but Woody was just a toy! Sid was definitely confused. How could a toy be talking by itself?

"It's busted," Sid said out loud.

"Who are you calling busted, Buster?" asked Woody.

Sid jumped. Woody *was* talking to him!

"That's right," Woody went on. "I'm talking to you, Sid Phillips. We don't like being blown up. We don't like being smashed or ripped apart."

"We?" Sid stared at Woody. The color drained from his face.

"That's right," said Woody. "Your toys."

As Woody spoke, the mutant toys rose up from the misty grass and the dusty haze of the backyard. They formed a circle around Sid.

"From now on," Woody instructed, "you must take good care of your toys."

Sid whimpered. His voice squeaked with fear.

"Play nice," Woody demanded. He whirled his head wildly on his neck. "We toys can see everything!"

That was enough for Sid. He dropped Woody and ran screaming into the house.

"The toys are alive!" he shouted.

We did it! We fixed the mean, nasty Sid. All the mutant toys rejoiced with us. Woody helped me off the pole and I held out my hand to my new friend.

"Thanks," I said.

Next door, Andy and his family were climbing into their van. The moving truck rumbled past.

"Quick!" cried Woody.

We had to catch them. After all we'd been through, we couldn't be left behind!

5. ☆ CHASE THAT TRUCK!

Woody and I ran to catch the van. It pulled out of the driveway and headed down the street. The moving truck followed close behind.

We raced across the yard. Scud was lying on Sid's porch. He bared his teeth when he saw us. Oh no! Not the dog again!

I sprinted to the back of the truck and caught hold of a strap that was hanging from the back door. I climbed up and called to Woody. He caught the strap, too, but Scud was close behind. He bit Woody's leg and clamped down.

"Hold on, Woody!" I cried.

"I can't," he yelled. Scud was tugging at his leg, pulling him down. "Take care of Andy for me!" Woody cried.

"Nooo!" I leaped off the truck and onto Scud's snout. Woody was my friend now. I couldn't leave him behind!

Scud yelped in pain.

While I fought the dog, Woody jumped into the back of the truck. He pushed past the boxes, looking for the ones that were Andy's. There! "Andy's Toys," read a box. Woody tore it open. As light flooded in, Slinky blinked his eyes. Mr. Potato Head looked around. Rex peered out, and so did Hamm the piggy bank. They all looked confused.

"Are we there yet?" they asked.

Woody couldn't find what he was looking for. He pushed their box aside and moved on to another one.

"Aha!" he cried. He found what he wanted—the car. He tossed it out the back of the truck and picked up the remote control, aiming the car at me. As it whizzed past, I jumped aboard. Woody turned it around and steered it back through traffic. I zipped through the stream of cars, leaving Scud far behind.

Once again, I was headed for the truck. I almost reached it, but Andy's toys scrambled out of their box.

"Look!" said Mr. Potato Head. "Woody's at it again!"

"No!" Woody tried to explain. "You don't understand! Buzz is out there! We've got to help him!"

The toys dove at Woody. "Get him!" cried Mr. Potato Head.

The toys lifted Woody high over their heads and tossed him out the back of the truck, heaving him into traffic.

In his hand, Woody clutched the remote control. The car caught up to him. Woody tumbled aboard.

"Thanks for the ride," he said.

With Woody at the controls, we sped toward the moving truck. Andy's toys had gathered at the back. They saw us zooming toward them.

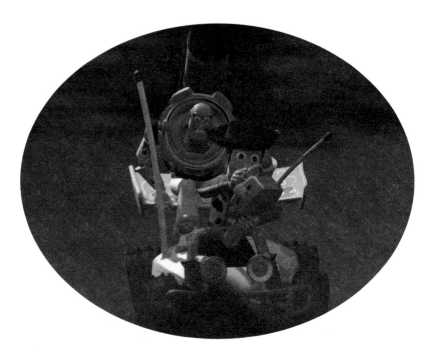

"Guys!" called Bo Peep. "Buzz *is* in the car with Woody! Woody was telling the truth!"

Now the toys knew they had to help.

They lowered the ramp so we could speed aboard. Closer. Our car was getting closer. Slinky stretched toward us and offered us his paw. Our car began to slow down.

"Speed up!" Woody cried.

"I can't!" I replied. "The batteries are running out!"

Slinky stretched longer and longer, trying to hang onto Woody's hand. But it was no use. We couldn't keep up. Slinky's paw slipped away from Woody, snapping back

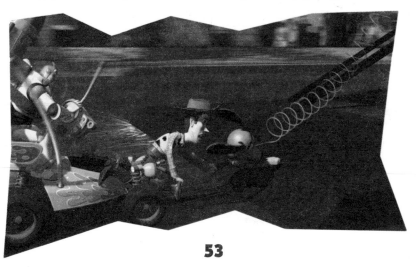

into the truck. Our car slowed to a stop as the truck barreled away. There was only one last hope, one last thing for us to try.

"The rocket!" cried Woody.

We still had the rocket that Sid had strapped to my back. Woody lit the fuse. The rocket hurtled us into traffic. We were moving faster than a spaceship as we streaked toward the truck and shot into the air. The fuse burned shorter. In seconds, the rocket would explode. The rocket cut loose as my space wings popped free. Woody held on as we flew through the air.

"Yahoo!" he cried. "You're flying! To infinity and beyond!"

Woody and I soared over the moving truck. In front of it was the van with Andy and his family. I dipped down and aimed for the sunroof. We fell into the backseat, right next to Andy. Perfect landing!

"Wow!" cried Andy as he picked us up. "It's Woody! And Buzz!"

His mother turned to see. "You found them," she said. "Where were they?"

"Right here!" said Andy. "In the car!"

As if we'd been there all along!

Above us, the rocket exploded. The sky lit up in a brilliant burst of color. The van sped down the highway, delivering us to our new home.

At the new house, Andy played with all of us. We didn't worry about whether he liked one toy more than another. Everything was peaceful.

Peaceful, that is, until Christmas.

Christmas morning, more presents arrived. Little Molly got a Mrs. Potato Head. Mr. Potato Head blushed. Now he would have a wife!

And Andy? He got a big package. A big, furry, wriggling package. He opened it. It was a puppy!

Hmmm. Did I say life was peaceful? It wouldn't be for long. I smiled at Woody and he smiled at me. Life might not be peaceful, but I was glad to be a toy. I no longer had to worry about fixing my spaceship and getting home. I had friends, and a boy who loved me. My space mission had been successful. I had found the happiest home of all.